The Bear Upstairs

by Shirley Mozelle

illustrated by
Doug Cushman

Henry Holt and Company • New York

Henry Holt and Company, LLC
Publishers since 1866
115 West 18th Street
New York, New York 10011
www.henryholt.com

Henry Holt is a registered trademark of Henry Holt and Company, LLC
Text copyright © 2005 by Shirley Mozelle
Illustrations copyright © 2005 by Doug Cushman
All rights reserved.
Distributed in Canada by H. B. Fenn and Company Ltd.

Library of Congress Cataloging-in-Publication Data
Mozelle, Shirley.
The bear upstairs / by Shirley Mozelle; illustrated by Doug Cushman.—1st ed.
p.   cm.
Summary: The downstairs bear is unhappy when the noisy upstairs bear moves in,
until she meets her neighbor and learns they have something in common.
ISBN-13: 978-0-8050-6820-7 / ISBN-10: 0-8050-6820-1
[1. Neighborliness—Fiction. 2. Bears—Fiction. 3. Cookery—Fiction.] I. Cushman, Doug, ill. II. Title.
PZ7.M868Be 2005   [E]—dc22   2004023392

First Edition—2005 / Designed Amy Manzo Toth
The artist used watercolor and pen and ink on Sanders watercolor paper,
with some colored-pencil additions, to create the art for this book.
Printed in the United States of America on acid-free paper. ∞

1 3 5 7 9 10 8 6 4 2

For Nina Ignatowicz,
Doug Cushman, Amy Manzo Toth, Robin Tordini,
and bears upstairs and down
—S. M.

To Clare, Xanthe, Michael, and Monty—
the bears upstairs
—D. C.

The upstairs bear moves in
on Wednesday.

Tables, books, chairs.
Boxes, boxes, boxes.

Klunk! Klunk!
   Bumpety-bump!
   Bump
        bump
           bump!

"I can't write like this,"
says the downstairs bear.
"I want Mrs. Solomon
to move back!"

BOOKS

That night at nine
the booping,
    bopping,
        klunking,
        bumping
stops.

"Ahhh!" sighs the
downstairs bear.

At ten o'clock
the upstairs bear takes
a shower.

"Me! Me! Me!
I'm a clean, clean bear!
I even wash my underwear!"

"Oh no!
Not a singing bear!"
says the downstairs bear
as she pulls a pillow
over her ears.

BOOKS

Suddenly,
CRASH!
Walls shake . . .

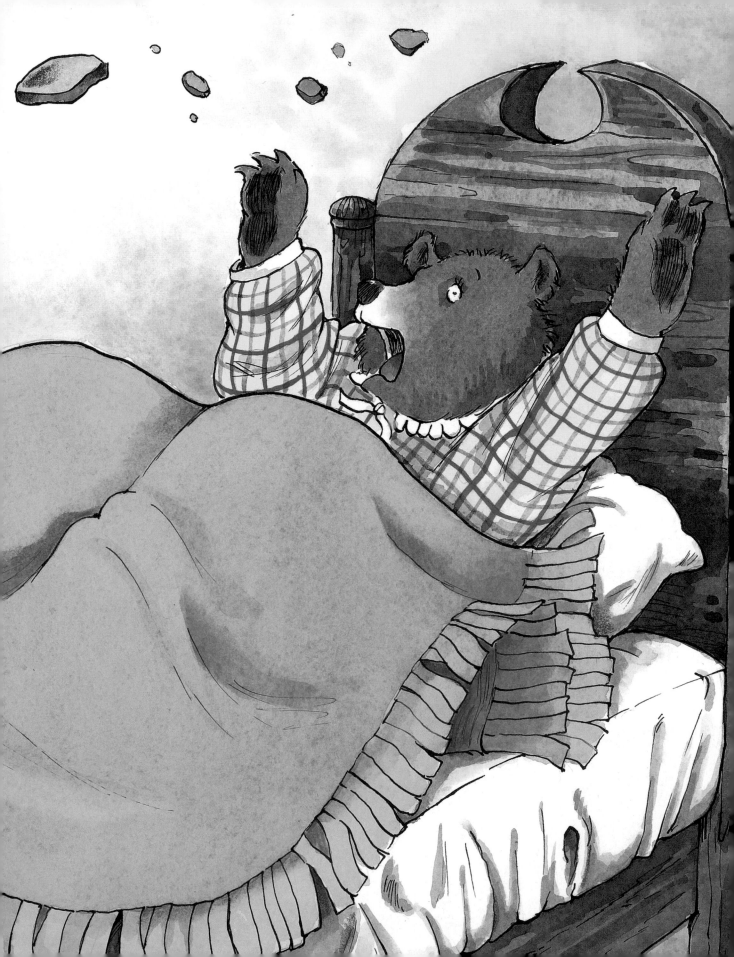

. . . then all is quiet.

Thursday morning at six,
the downstairs bear wakes.
She fixes tea, toast,
then sits down
in her favorite chair
to write.
    Type-type!
      Click-click!
Then . . .

Thump-thump!
   Bump-bump!

The upstairs bear is up.
He has coffee, doughnuts,
unpacks his boxes—
toothbrush, comb,
soap, shampoo, towels,
sheets, pillowcases, blankets.
He hangs shirts, ties,
pants, coats
in the closet.

Bip! Bop!
 Roll! Bang!

Shoes, baseball,
softball, bat,
glove, bowling ball.

 Bim-bam-boom!

The downstairs bear
straightens pictures
on the wall.
She feeds Arthur.

The upstairs bear unpacks
dishes, glasses,
forks, spoons,
bowls, knives,
pots, skillets,
juicer, colander,
omelet maker.

**Klink-tink!
Tinkety-
klink!**

The downstairs bear
has another cup of tea.

The upstairs bear
turns on the radio.
   Win a trip to Honolulu!
After a while the radio stops.
Then . . .

Rumba-mambo-samba!

The upstairs bear dances.
Dust falls from the ceiling.

"A dancing bear!"
gasps the downstairs bear.

The downstairs bear walks up the stairs.

Knock! Knock! Knock!

Nothing.

Knock! Knock! Knock! KNOCK!

The door opens, and a friendly face smiles at her.
"I live downstairs," the downstairs bear says.
"I'm so glad to meet you!" says the upstairs bear.
He pulls her gently inside and turns off the music.

Cookbooks are everywhere—
Basting, Broiling, Baking.
Veggie Tarts, Veggie Noodles.
Fish and How to Buy Them.
And there is HER book!
Veggie Poems for Bears.

"Stay for lunch!"
"I can't. . . ."
"Sure you can. We're neighbors!"
says the upstairs bear. "I love your
recipe for Anytime Omelet."
"You do?" says the downstairs bear.

Chop-Chop!
Crack-Crack!

Eggs in a bowl. Salt, pepper, a little vanilla.
"I heard you typing this morning,"
says the upstairs bear.
"You heard ME?" asks the downstairs bear.
"Music is everywhere," says the upstairs bear.
"Pipes sing. Walls talk. Kettles whistle."
   Hummmm-humm-hummm! He hums.
And floors holler, the downstairs bear thinks.

"I start work at Lloyd's Café as a chef on Monday!"
says the upstairs bear.
"Monday?" says the downstairs bear.
"Monday," says the upstairs bear.

Whip! Stir! Swish!

Hummmm-humm-hummm!

The downstairs bear picks up the tune—
hummmm-humm—
and places plates on the table.

In the skillet, a hot butter sizzle.